Joy the Summer Vacation Fairy

For Olivia Cowle

Special thanks to Linda Chapman

ISBN 978-0-439-93442-8

Previously published as *Summer the Holiday Fairy*
by Orchard U.K. in 2005.

25 24 23 17/0
Printed in the U.S.A. 40

First Scholastic printing, May 2007

Joy the Summer Vacation Fairy

by Daisy Meadows

SCHOLASTIC INC.
New York Toronto London Auckland
Sydney Mexico City New Delhi Hong Kong

The Fairyland Palace
Maze
Forest
Orchard
Meadow
Tower
Donkey Rides
Beach
Tidepools
Rainspell Island

Jack Frost's
Ice Castle
Jack Frost's
Sandcastle
Stream
Field
rmaid
tage
Town
Underwater
Cave
Harbor
Rosie's
Rosie's
Ice cream
Truck
Dolphin Cottage

Come wind, come breeze,
Come howling gale;
Whip up waves and billow sail!
Gather all the shells and sand
From every corner of the land.

And with my special breezy spells
I'll steal the magic Rainspell Shells.
Then beaches, ice cream, summer fun
Will be spoiled for everyone!

Find the hidden letters in the shells throughout this book. Unscramble all 3 letters to spell a special word!

Joy the Summer Vacation Fairy

The Curly Twirly Shell

The Fairy Footprint 1

A Sudden Storm 11

Where Did All the Sand Go? 25

Jack Frost's Palace 35

The Magic Shell 47

"Have you finished packing yet, Rachel?" Mrs. Walker called up the stairs. "Kirsty and her parents will be here soon."

"Almost done!" Rachel Walker shouted back. It was the beginning of summer vacation and, in just a few hours, she and her parents would be back

on Rainspell Island! Even better, Kirsty Tate, Rachel's best friend, was going to be staying there with her parents, too. The two girls had met on that same island the summer before. It had been a magical time!

Very magical, Rachel thought with a smile. She and Kirsty shared an amazing secret. They were friends with the fairies! They had first met the fairies when the king and queen of Fairyland asked for their help rescuing the Rainbow Fairies. Since then, Rachel and Kirsty had had many more fairy adventures.

I wonder if we'll see any fairies this summer, Rachel thought. She touched the golden locket she always wore around her neck. Kirsty had one just like it. They had been

gifts from the Fairy Queen, and were filled with magical fairy dust!

Rachel only had two things left to pack — her toothbrush and her favorite T-shirt. She hunted through her drawers. Where was it? Just then, she glimpsed the corner of a sleeve sticking out from under her bed.

"Oh, no!" she groaned, pulling the shirt out. There was a big ketchup stain on the front.

Upset that she hadn't asked her mom to wash it earlier, Rachel went to the bathroom to get her toothbrush.

When she came back, she gasped. The T-shirt was neatly folded on the bed, and the big stain had nearly disappeared! There was just one little mark on the sleeve.

Rachel leaned in to take a closer look. It wasn't just a mark. It was . . . a tiny, sandy footprint!

A ray of sunshine shone through the window, and the sleeve of her T-shirt glowed.

"Fairy dust!" Rachel breathed.

But the magical moment was interrupted when a car beeped outside.

"Hurry up, Rachel!" Rachel heard her mom's footsteps on the stairs. "Kirsty's here."

Rachel shoved the T-shirt in her suitcase and hurried downstairs.

"Hi, Rachel!" Kirsty cried, running through the front door. Her dark hair was in pigtails, and she was wearing shorts and a pink T-shirt.

"Sorry, we're a little late!" Mrs. Tate, Kirsty's mom, said as she and Mr.

Tate walked in, behind Kirsty. "The car had a flat tire when we got up this morning."

"Or at least I thought it did," Mr. Tate added. "But by the time I'd gotten my tools out, the tire wasn't flat anymore. Very strange." He laughed. "Almost like magic."

Rachel and Kirsty exchanged looks. Magic!

Rachel wanted to tell Kirsty about the fairy footprint, but she couldn't say anything in front of their parents. "Um, Kirsty, do you want to come and see my new comforter before we leave?"

"Sure," Kirsty replied.

They ran upstairs. Kirsty seemed to realize that the comforter had just been an excuse.

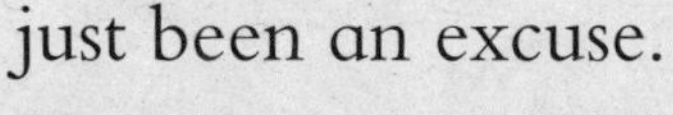

She glanced quickly at it. "It's beautiful," she said before turning back to Rachel, her eyes shining. "So, do you think my dad's tire was fixed by magic? It was really weird. I was with Dad when he went back with his tools and I thought I heard some music — it was like the bells on an ice cream truck."

Rachel couldn't hold her news in any longer. "I bet it was magic!" she said. "A fairy's been here, too."

"Really?" Kirsty gasped.

Rachel nodded and told Kirsty about her T-shirt. "There was a tiny, sandy footprint on it," she said. "It must have been made by a fairy."

"Let's look around!" Kirsty exclaimed. "Maybe the fairy's still here!"

Rachel and Kirsty had just started looking when Mr. Walker opened the door. "Come on, you two. If we don't leave now, we'll miss the ferry."

The girls took one last look around Rachel's bedroom, then followed Mr. Walker downstairs. They piled in Rachel's dad's car and set off for the ferry.

The girls couldn't talk about fairies with Mr. and Mrs. Walker sitting in the front seat, but it was fun just to be together again.

"I can't wait to get to Rainspell Island," Rachel said, grinning.

"Me, neither," agreed Kirsty. "I want some of Rosie's Rainspell ice cream."

"Yum!" Rachel sighed happily. Rosie sold delicious ice cream from her truck near the harbor. "I can't wait to go swimming at the beach."

"And wade in the tidepools," Kirsty said.

They grinned at each other. Their vacation was going to be so much fun!

As they got on the ferry, Mr. Tate looked up at the blue sky. "It should be a very calm trip," he commented.

"Good," said Mrs. Walker. "I don't want to feel seasick!"

While the ferry chugged across the flat blue water, Rachel and Kirsty watched eagerly for a glimpse of Rainspell Island.

"There it is!" Kirsty exclaimed as a rocky island appeared on the horizon. Suddenly,

she shivered. "*Brrr.* The sun went behind a cloud!"

The girls looked up. Big black clouds were racing across the sky.

"The sea's getting rougher," Rachel said.

"Wow, what a quick change in the weather!" Mr. Tate exclaimed.

"Do you think it's magic?" Rachel whispered to Kirsty.

"Maybe it has something to do with Jack Frost," Kirsty whispered back. The ferry lurched over a wave, and she grabbed on to her seat.

"I don't feel very well," Mrs. Walker said, looking green. "I think I'd better go inside. Are you coming, girls?"

"No, we'll stay out here," Rachel said. The waves were really choppy now and the wind was freezing, but she wanted to talk to Kirsty alone.

"OK, but if it gets any rougher I want you both to come inside," replied Mrs. Walker.

"It has to be magic!" Kirsty said to Rachel as soon as their parents had left.

"I bet Jack Frost is up to something," Rachel replied.

The waves got rougher and rougher.

"I think we should go inside," said Kirsty, looking worried.

Rachel nodded. Holding on to nearby seats, they staggered toward the door.

Suddenly, a big wave tossed the boat upward. Kirsty stumbled and fell, landing next to a pile of ropes.

Fighting to keep her balance, Rachel hurried after her friend. "Are you OK?"

Kirsty nodded. "Yes, thanks."

As she started to get up, Rachel grabbed her arm. "What's that?"

"What?" Kirsty asked.

"That noise," said Rachel. "Listen!"

They both listened. They could hear a tiny groaning sound coming from somewhere nearby. And one of the coils of rope looked a little glittery, even though the sun wasn't shining.

"It's coming from over here!" Kirsty said. "It's . . ." She broke off with a gasp. "Oh!"

There was a fairy lying under the rope! She had shoulder-length honey-blond hair and was wearing a bright top and a matching skirt. She had a necklace made out of tiny, white shells. Her skin was pale under her freckles. She groaned and clutched her stomach.

"Hello," Rachel said softly.

The fairy jumped. For a moment, she looked scared, but then she smiled. "Oh, hello! Aren't you Rachel and Kirsty?" she asked.

"Yes!" Rachel replied. She felt a thrill of excitement that the fairy knew who they were.

"I'm Joy the Summer Vacation Fairy," the little fairy told them. "I make sure that summer vacations are special. I . . ." She broke off with a moan.

"Are you OK?" Kirsty asked.

"No, I feel awfully seasick!" said Joy. "It's all Jack Frost's fault. He turned the sea rough."

Kirsty looked at Rachel. "We *thought* it was Jack Frost!"

"He's been doing all sorts of bad things on Rainspell Island," Joy said weakly.

Rachel frowned. "Like what?"

Joy moaned again. "I'm sorry, I can't tell you right now. I feel too sick! If I didn't feel so bad, I could use my magic seaweed to calm the waves."

"Can we help?" said Kirsty.

Joy nodded and opened her fairy-size beach bag, which was covered with tiny embroidered shells. She pulled out a strand of seaweed that glittered with green sparkles. "Slide this over the top of the waves, and the water will calm down."

Rachel and Kirsty hurried to the side of the ferry. Rachel leaned over the railing, but the waves still looked far away.

"It's not going to reach," Rachel said in dismay, dangling the piece of seaweed from her hand. Then she gasped. "Kirsty, look!"

The sparkly seaweed was growing!

"Wow!" Kirsty exclaimed.

The seaweed stretched down and down until it brushed the top of the waves. With a

whoosh, a burst of green-and-gold sparks fizzed across the water. Almost immediately, the waves began to calm.

"It's working!" Kirsty cried.

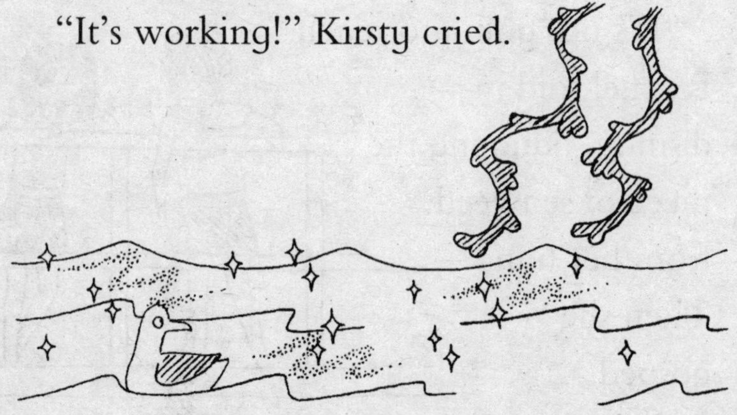

They pulled up the seaweed and ran back to Joy. The little fairy was smoothing down her wavy hair. "Thank you so much," she said. "I'm feeling better already!" She grinned at them. "Did you notice that I was at your houses today?"

"You cleaned my T-shirt!" Rachel said.

"And fixed my dad's tire!" Kirsty added.

Joy nodded. "I was trying to make sure Jack Frost didn't keep you from getting to Rainspell on time. I really need your help. The goblins have been wrecking everyone's vacations because Jack Frost wants Rainspell Island all for himself."

Her wand suddenly made a tinkling sound, like the bells on an ice cream truck.

Kirsty nudged Rachel. "That's the noise I heard when my dad's tire was being fixed!"

"Oh, goodness!" Joy exclaimed, looking at her wand. "There must be a new problem on the island. I'll tell you all about Jack Frost later. Thanks for helping me!"

She flew into the air in a burst of golden dust. The next second, she was gone.

Rachel beamed at Kirsty. "It looks like we're going to be having a fairy adventure this summer after all!"

Where Did All the Sand Go?

When the ferry arrived at Rainspell Island, the sky was blue again and the waves lapped gently in the harbor.

Rachel skipped off the boat in excitement. Even if Jack Frost was causing trouble, it was still wonderful to be back on the island.

Kirsty was feeling the same way. "This is going to be the best vacation ever!" she declared.

But they soon noticed that something was very wrong. Usually, everyone on Rainspell Island looked happy, but now everyone was very glum. Even the seagulls were sitting gloomily on the harbor wall, instead of swooping joyfully through the sky.

"I wonder why everyone looks so sad," said Mrs. Walker.

As soon as they reached the beach, they found out.

There was no sand! Instead of the soft golden beach, there were just dull gray pebbles and sharp rocks.

"What happened?" exclaimed Mrs. Tate.

"All the sand just disappeared," said a man passing by. "A storm came through

and, when it was over, the sand was all gone."

Kirsty and Rachel exchanged horrified looks. Was this Jack Frost's work?

"Oh, dear," Mrs. Walker said. "I guess you won't be building any sand castles today, girls."

"Never mind," said Mr. Tate, trying to be cheerful. "It's not the end of the world. I'm sure everything else on the island will still be perfect. Let's go and get some ice cream."

But when they reached the ice cream truck, they saw a big sign on it that said CLOSED.

A woman with curly red hair was locking the truck. "Rosie!" Kirsty called, recognizing the ice cream lady from the summer before.

The girls ran over to Rosie. "Are you about to open the truck?" Rachel asked.

Rosie shook her head. "I don't have any ice cream," she said. "It's been

melting as soon as I make it, and I can't figure out why. A few people tried drinking it like soup, but it tasted horrible — all salty, like seawater." She sighed. "I don't know what's wrong, but nothing I've tried has made any difference."

"Oh, goodness!" Mrs. Walker exclaimed. "No sand, no ice cream. This isn't going to be much of a vacation."

Rachel and Kirsty looked at each other. They couldn't believe it!

"We'll be fine," said Rachel's dad, seeing the girls' faces. He pointed to a flyer on a nearby

lamppost. "Look, there's a sailing regatta in a few days. That should be fun!"

"I guess so," Mrs. Walker agreed, cheering up a little.

But Rachel and Kirsty weren't so sure. If Jack Frost was really determined to spoil everyone's vacation, who knew what he'd do next?

As soon as they'd gone to their cottages and finished unpacking, Rachel and Kirsty went for a walk on the beach. It was quiet and lonely! There were no people sunbathing or playing games.

Kirsty looked for a flat stone to skip across the water. As she picked one up, a shower of golden dust flew into the air.

"Oh!" Kirsty and Rachel gasped as Joy twirled up into the sky.

"Hi, there!" called the fairy. "I was just helping a hermit crab. The shell on its back got whisked away by Jack Frost's magic. It didn't have anywhere to live. Look!"

A sad-looking hermit crab was shuffling sideways toward a little hut built out of twigs.

"I built it a house," Joy explained. "But I think it would rather have its shell back."

"Has Jack Frost taken all the shells?" Kirsty asked.

Joy nodded.

"Why?" Rachel said.

"I'll show you." Joy raised her golden wand, and a cloud of glittering fairy dust and tiny shells swirled down. It smelled like sunscreen and ice cream. As the fairy dust landed on Rachel and Kirsty, they felt themselves shrinking.

"We're fairy-size again!" they cried happily.

Kirsty and Rachel fluttered their new fairy wings and soared up into the sky with Joy. Fairy dust glimmered in the air behind them.

"This way!" Joy said.

Rachel and Kirsty followed her as she swooped over the forest to the other side of the island. "There's the maze!" Rachel

exclaimed as they flew over some green hedges laid out in a twisty pattern.

"And the ruined tower!" Kirsty pointed to a crumbling stack of stone. The girls remembered it well from last summer.

"Almost there!" Joy called.

At a place where the forest met the beach, she dived down and landed.

Rachel and Kirsty stared. Half-hidden at the edge of the trees was the most enormous sand castle they had ever seen. It was decorated with thousands and thousands of shells. A large moat had been built around it, and four ugly goblins with long noses and big feet stood guard.

"So that's where all the sand and shells have gone!" Kirsty said, looking at the castle's shell-studded walls in surprise.

"Yes," replied Joy. "Jack Frost went to the sand castle competition on the beach last week. He cast a spell to turn the winning castle into a giant palace for his summer vacation. It was so big, he needed all the sand and shells from the beach." She shook her head. "Worst of all, he stole the three special Rainspell Shells from their cave under the sea."

"What are the Rainspell Shells?" Rachel asked.

"They're magic shells that make Rainspell Island the best place ever for vacation," Joy explained. "The first is a long pink-and-cream spiral shell. It makes all the food on Rainspell Island, like Rosie's ice cream, taste extra-delicious. The second is a beautiful conch shell that controls the wind and waves, making the sea perfect for sailing and swimming. The third is a huge scallop shell. That one makes sure that all of the beaches on Rainspell have sand and that all of the tidepools are full of beautiful shells. If I could return all three shells to their cave, then Jack Frost's palace would vanish and Rainspell Island would be back to normal

again." She looked anxiously at the two girls. "Do you think you could help me?"

"Of course!" Rachel and Kirsty said.

Joy smiled. "Thank you so much!" Her smile faded. "Though I'm not sure how we can do it."

Kirsty looked at Jack Frost's castle. "Let's fly closer and see if we can find any of the magic shells."

Rachel nodded. "But we'd better be careful of those goblins." The girls had learned that goblins were mean and horrible. They would do anything to please Jack Frost.

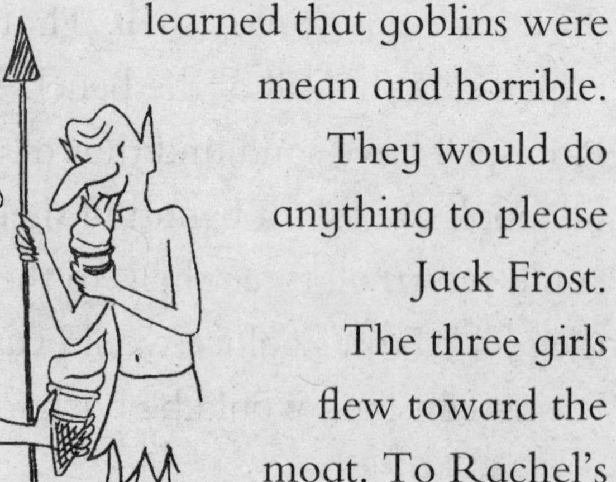

The three girls flew toward the moat. To Rachel's

and Kirsty's relief, the goblins seemed to be too busy eating ice cream to be searching the sky.

"Where did they get that ice cream?" Kirsty whispered.

Joy sighed. "They made it themselves. Since they have the shell that makes Rainspell's food taste yummy, they can make Rosie's special ice cream. Jack Frost is pleased, because it means that he and his goblins are the only ones on the island who can have Rosie's ice cream."

Only one of the goblins — the one who was defending the castle's drawbridge — didn't have any ice cream. "Come on, give me some of

yours," he grumbled to another goblin. "I can't leave the drawbridge to get my own, or Jack Frost will be angry."

"Well, you can't have any of mine!" the other goblin shouted back.

"Mmm, this is delicious!" another one teased. "In fact, it's the best ice cream I've ever tasted! Mmmm."

The drawbridge goblin stamped his foot. The other goblins walked off, laughing.

The goblin by the drawbridge was so angry that he hit the castle wall with his fist, almost knocking off a large, twirly pink-and-cream shell.

"That goblin doesn't look very happy," Rachel commented.

Kirsty didn't reply. She was too busy staring at the castle. "Look, Joy! The pink twisty shell," she breathed, pointing. "Isn't it one of the three magic shells?"

"Yes!" Joy exclaimed. "It is!"

Rachel eyed the big, scary goblin nearby. "But how are we going to get it back?"

"We could wait until the goblin leaves," Kirsty suggested.

"We could be waiting for a long time," Rachel pointed out.

"If only we could make the goblin move," said Joy.

"Maybe he'll decide he can't wait for some ice cream any longer," Rachel

said hopefully. "And he'll leave the drawbridge."

"That's it!" Kirsty gasped. Rachel and Joy looked at her. "You two could tell the goblin you have some ice cream on the other side of that sand dune. When he leaves to follow you, I'll fly down and grab the magic shell."

"That's a great idea!" Rachel said.

Joy nodded. "Come on! Let's go!"

The Magic Shell

Kirsty hovered in the air as Rachel and Joy flew toward the goblin.

"Hey!" he shouted as they swooped down. "What are you doing? Jack Frost said I cannot let any fairies into the palace!" He tried to grab Joy out of the air, but she darted away.

"We're not trying to get into the castle,"

Rachel said, her heart pounding. The goblin looked even scarier close up. "We just wanted to tell you that there's some ice cream on the other side of that sand dune."

The goblin frowned. "What sort of ice cream?"

"It's a special, extra-delicious flavor that no one else here has tasted," Joy said.

The goblin looked interested. "Does it have chocolate sauce and sprinkles?"

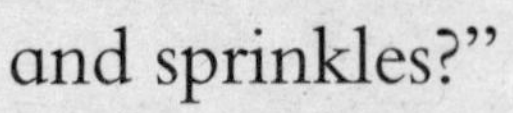

"Oh, yes," said Rachel. "*Lots* of sprinkles."

"I guess I could just run over to the

other side of the sand dune for a minute," said the goblin. Then he shook his head. "I bet you fairies are trying to trick me. You just want to get into the castle!" He waved his hands at them. "Go away! Leave me alone!"

Joy and Rachel flew away in alarm.

"Did it work?" Kirsty asked, joining them.

"No," Rachel said with a sigh. "He realized that we were trying to trick him."

"Hmmm . . ." Joy said, her eyes lighting up, "what

if we make him believe we really *do* have ice cream?"

"But how can we do that?" asked Rachel.

Joy grinned. "Like this!" She waved her wand. There was a loud splatting noise, and two blobs of melted ice cream flew through the air. One landed on Rachel's T-shirt, and another on Joy's skirt.

"Sorry!" Joy said, seeing the surprised look on Rachel's

face. "I know it's sticky, but it might convince the goblin that we have some ice cream."

"But I thought the goblins had all the ice cream magic," said Kirsty, puzzled.

"They have the magic that makes the ice cream *taste* great," Joy explained. "I can still make ice cream, just like Rosie can. It's just all melted and sticky and tastes horrible." She looked at Rachel. "So what do you think?"

Rachel grinned. "I think it might just work!"

They flew down to the goblin again.

"I told you to go away!" he grumbled as they hovered just out of reach.

"I know. We tried to bring the ice cream to you, but there's too much to carry," said Rachel. "Look, it spilled all over our clothes."

The goblin peered at her T-shirt. "So there really *is* ice cream over there?"

"Yes," Rachel replied. "But it's melting fast!"

The goblin jumped to his feet. "Show me where it is — quickly!"

Rachel and Joy flew toward the dune. The goblin ran behind them, licking his lips.

Kirsty saw her chance. Swooping down, she landed beside the pink-and-cream spiral shell on the drawbridge. She tried to pull it off, but it was much heavier than she'd expected.

Come on, she thought frantically. She pulled harder.

"Quick, Kirsty!"

Kirsty looked around. Rachel and Joy were flying toward her at top speed. The goblin was right behind them. He must have realized he'd been tricked when there wasn't any ice cream on the other side of the dune.

Kirsty gave the shell one last tug. To her relief, it popped out of the sand. She held it with both hands and flew into the air, escaping just in time.

"Hooray!" shouted Joy.

"You tricky fairies!" cried the goblin. "Come back here with that shell!"

Joy sped away, with Kirsty and Rachel right behind her. As the girls flew over trees, the goblin's voice grew fainter.

"Won't Jack Frost be really angry when he hears what happened?" Kirsty said.

Joy nodded. "We're going to have to be extra-careful. Now he knows that we're after the Rainspell Shells." She pointed at the twirly curly shell. "At least we have one of them back.

Come on, I'll show you the underwater cave."

Kirsty glanced at Rachel. "We should really be getting back."

"Yes," Rachel agreed. "We told our parents we were only going for a short walk."

"Never mind," Joy replied. "You can always come and see the cave another time. After all, we still have two more magic shells to find!" She flew up into the air. "See you soon!" Before she swooped away, she flicked her wand and the girls grew to their normal size again.

Rachel and Kirsty waved good-bye and

headed back to the beach.

"That was fun!" Rachel said.

As she spoke, a shimmering haze waved through the air. They heard the faint sound of ice cream bells.

"Something magical is happening!" Kirsty exclaimed.

"Maybe Joy is putting the shell back?" Rachel suggested.

As soon as they reached the road, they heard ice cream bells again. "More magic?" Rachel said.

"No!" Kirsty cried. "Look!"

Rosie's ice cream truck was driving along the road. "Hello, you two," Rosie called. "Great news! My ice cream machine is working again. In fact, the ice cream tastes even better than before!"

"That's fantastic!" Rachel said.

Rosie nodded. "I'm so happy, I've decided to give out free ice cream all afternoon. Would you like some?"

"Yes, please!" Rachel and Kirsty said at the same time.

Rachel chose chocolate ice cream and Kirsty chose strawberry.

"Mmm, this really *is* delicious!" Rachel said. "Thanks, Rosie!"

"No problem." Rosie smiled at the girls before driving away.

Kirsty licked her cone. "Isn't it wonderful that Rosie's ice cream is back to normal?"

Rachel nodded. "Yes, but we still need to do something about the sand and the seashells."

"We'll have to help Joy rescue the other Rainspell Shells," Kirsty said.

"Definitely," Rachel vowed. "We'll make Rainspell Island the perfect place for a vacation again. I just know we will!"

The Sea Breeze Shell

What Happened to the Wind? 65

The Goblin Regatta 75

Jack Frost 87

Sally's Tunnel 101

Escape! 117

What Happened to the Wind?

"Isn't it a beautiful day for the regatta?" Kirsty asked as she put on her sneakers.

Rachel looked out the window of Dolphin Cottage. There wasn't a cloud in the sky. "It's perfect," she replied. "My dad's really excited."

Mr. Walker and Mr. Tate were renting

a boat and racing at the regatta that morning.

Kirsty dropped her voice to a whisper. "At least Jack Frost won't be able to ruin today. It won't make a difference to the regatta if there aren't any shells or sand on the beach."

A shiver ran across Rachel's skin as she thought about Jack Frost. She and Kirsty still had to help Joy the Summer Vacation Fairy rescue two of the Rainspell Shells. "Do you think we'll see Joy today?" she asked.

"I hope so!" Kirsty said, grinning widely.

The Walkers and the Tates walked to the harbor together.

"Goodness, it's hot," Mrs. Walker said.

Mr. Tate wiped his hand across his forehead. "I hope a breeze picks up. If there's no wind, then the boats won't be able to sail."

"It's very strange," Kirsty's mom said. "It was so windy when we came over on the ferry the other day!"

Rachel and Kirsty hurried ahead of

their parents. "Are you thinking what I'm thinking?" Kirsty whispered.

"That it could be Jack Frost?" Rachel said. "Maybe he *is* going to ruin the regatta, after all!"

Just then, their parents caught up with them. The pretty streets that led down to the harbor were filled with crowds of people. Everyone looked hot and worried, and there was a long line by Rosie's ice cream truck.

"There's the harbor master." Mr. Walker pointed to a man dressed in a blue uniform. "He's in charge of the regatta. Let's find out what's going on."

The harbor master was talking to a group of people by the dock. "I'm very sorry," he was saying. "If the wind doesn't pick up in the next half hour, I'm afraid the regatta will be canceled."

There were groans from the crowd.

Kirsty and Rachel glanced at each other. They needed to do something, and fast!

"Can Kirsty and I go to the beach, please?" Rachel asked.

"Sure," replied Mrs. Walker. "Meet us by Rosie's truck in half an hour. If the

race is taking place, we can watch it together."

"And if it isn't, we can all go home," Mr. Tate said gloomily.

Rachel and Kirsty wriggled through the crowd and made their way onto the beach. They hurried across the pebbles until they were out of earshot.

"We have to do something!" Kirsty

said. "I'm sure this is Jack Frost's fault. Doesn't he have the magic shell that controls the wind?"

Rachel nodded. "I bet he's trying to ruin everyone's day!" As she spoke, her foot knocked against a piece of driftwood. There was a happy tinkling sound, and a fountain of golden sparks exploded into the air.

"Joy!" Rachel and Kirsty exclaimed as the fairy flew out from under the driftwood and twirled into the sky.

"Hi, there!" said Joy, smoothing

down her ruffled skirt and grinning at them. "How are you today?"

"Not great," Rachel admitted. "There's no wind, so it looks like the regatta's going to be canceled. Everyone's really upset."

Joy frowned. "Oh, it's all Jack Frost's fault! He's using the magic shell. He brought all the wind over to his side of the island for *his* regatta." She put her hands on her hips. "He is so mean!"

"Can we do anything to stop him?" asked Kirsty.

"The only way we

can stop him is by getting that conch shell back," Joy replied. "Jack Frost put it on one of the towers of his castle. If we can find it, then he won't be able to control the wind anymore."

Rachel and Kirsty exchanged determined looks. "Then let's go back to the castle!" they said.

The Goblin Regatta

Joy waved her wand, and a cloud of golden dust floated over the girls. Within seconds, they were fairy-size again. They flew over the woods and the tower, and then arrived at Jack Frost's sandcastle.

Loud shouts were coming from the direction of the beach.

"What's that noise?" Rachel wondered aloud.

"I bet it's the goblins," Joy answered, frowning.

They swooped over the castle to investigate.

The goblins were sailing on the sea in a strange assortment of inflatable toys, with sails made out of beach towels and

tablecloths. The boats bounced across the waves, only stopping when they knocked into one another. Half the goblins seemed to be in the water. The others were yelling at one another. A tall goblin with a megaphone was standing on the beach shouting instructions, but everyone was ignoring him.

Kirsty looked back at the castle. It had three towers, a tall one in the middle and two shorter ones on either side. The top of each tower was decorated with conch shells, which were creamy-brown on the outside and glossy-pink inside.

"Which one is the magic shell that controls the wind?" Kirsty asked.

"It's on the tower to the left." Joy pointed. "I think it's the shell with the brown stripes." She frowned. "Or maybe it's the one with the beige spots. No, no, I think it might be the large cream shell with no markings."

Rachel frowned. If Joy didn't know which shell it was, how could they possibly rescue the right one? "We have to know which shell it is," she said anxiously.

"Yes, Rachel's right," Kirsty added.

"Don't worry," Joy said, glancing at the sky. "I think we'll find out any minute now!"

Just then, the sun suddenly came out from behind a cloud. As its rays fell on the towers, one of the shells began to glow.

"Oh, wow!" Kirsty breathed. "That *has* to be the magic shell!"

"It is," Joy said. "It always glitters in the sun. The question is, how are we going to rescue it? We can't just fly up and grab it. Jack Frost might see us." She pointed to a

window near the top of the middle tower. "He can't come outside, because he'd melt in the sun. So he watches everything from that window. He could see us flying up to the tower!" She ran a hand through her blond hair. "I think the only way to get the shell is by going up through the inside of the castle. Then we can take the shell and sneak away."

"But what if Jack Frost notices that the shell is missing before we get away?" asked Kirsty.

Rachel glanced out at the beach. She had an idea! "If we found a shell that

looked like the magic shell, we could swap them! Then Jack Frost wouldn't know we'd taken it, and we could escape before he figured it out."

"Oh, yes!" Kirsty said.

Joy beamed. "Great idea! Let's go!"

The three girls flew down to the beach, staying in the shadow of the castle walls. Luckily, none of the goblins noticed them — the creatures were too busy squabbling in their boats.

"How are we going to get into the castle?" Kirsty asked.

"Let's hide under this seaweed while we decide what to do," suggested Rachel. It was scary being on the beach with so many goblins around, especially when she was fairy-size. She lifted up a strand of seaweed.

"Hey!" a voice exclaimed. A large hermit crab without a shell glared at them from under the seaweed. "That was keeping me warm," it said, snapping its claws.

Rachel and Kirsty backed away. "Oh, I'm sorry . . ." Rachel stammered.

"Henry!" cried Joy. To Rachel and Kirsty's surprise, Joy hurried over and threw her arms around the crab. Smiling broadly, she turned to them. "Didn't I tell you about Henry? I built him a house because he'd lost his shell."

"Oh, yes!" Kirsty and Rachel both exclaimed.

"Henry, this is Kirsty and Rachel," Joy said. "They're helping me get the Rainspell Shells back. I'm sorry we moved your seaweed, but we were trying to hide so the goblins wouldn't see us."

"Oh," Henry said. "I'm sorry if I was a little bit snappy just now, but I hate not

having a shell. That's why I came here, to Jack Frost's beach. I thought I might find myself another one."

"There are tons of shells over here," said Rachel, turning around to tug at the seaweed. She stopped with a gasp. "Hide! Jack Frost is looking out of the tower!"

Jack Frost

A tall, bony figure was staring out of the window at the top of the tallest tower. His spiky hair stood out around his head, and his beard was frozen into icicles. As he gazed around, the girls and Joy ducked down under the seaweed.

"Why aren't you racing?" Jack Frost shouted angrily to the goblins below.

Looking panicked, one goblin raised his megaphone. "Race, everyone!" he shouted. "Race!"

Immediately, all of the goblins tried to sail in different directions. Four of the boats crashed into one another, and two tipped over.

Splash! The goblins fell into the sea!

Grabbing a sun hat, Jack Frost shoved it on his head and leaned out of the window. "Ridiculous goblins! You couldn't entertain an icicle! Do something else. Play me some music, instead. The goblin who plays me the best music will get as much candy as he can eat."

"Candy!" the goblins murmured greedily.

"The rest of you will get" — Jack Frost grinned nastily at the hopeful goblins — "absolutely nothing!"

Laughing, he ducked back inside his tower.

The goblins on the beach scrambled around, grabbing anything they could use for a musical instrument. They banged on upside-down buckets and blew into shells as if they were horns. Rachel, Kirsty, and Joy clapped their hands over their ears. The noise was terrible! Rachel realized that this was their chance.

The goblins were all so busy that the back door of the castle was completely unguarded. "Quick!" she hissed. "Let's sneak in while they're not looking."

"We need to find a shell that looks like the magic shell first," Joy pointed out.

"There are some over there." Kirsty pointed to where a group of goblins was arguing over a pile of conch shells.

A goblin with a big wart at the end of his nose was holding a beautiful cream shell.

"I want that one!" grumbled one of the other goblins.

"Well, you can't have it! It's mine!"

Clutching the shell, the warty-nosed goblin hurried away. He sat down on the sand near the girls and started blowing into the shell. A few strangled toots came out.

The goblin shook the shell and tried again.

"That shell would be perfect," Kirsty breathed. "It looks just like the magic shell!"

"Yes," agreed Rachel, watching the goblin. "But we need to convince him to give it to us!"

Just then, Henry scuttled out from under the seaweed. "That looks like it might be a good shell for me," he said, heading toward a yellow-and-white shell nearby. Then he shook his head. "No," he said, sighing. "Its end is too pointy. Pointy shells are not comfortable homes. They're good for blowing in, but not for living in."

Joy gasped. "Oh, Henry, you just gave me an idea! Let's get the goblin to trade his conch shell for that pointy shell."

"How?" Kirsty asked.

Joy grinned. "With a little bit of magic, of course!"

She waved her wand, filling the air with golden sparkles and tiny, glittering shells. As they fell on the pointy shell, the faint sound of a merry-go-round echoed through the air.

The goblin looked up. "What's that?"

"I've enchanted the shell so that it makes summery music," Joy whispered to

Rachel and Kirsty. Picking up the shell, she flew over to the goblin. "Excuse me!" she called.

Rachel and Kirsty joined her. Was this going to work?

The goblin frowned. "We're not supposed to let fairies anywhere near the castle. Get lost!"

"But we brought you a shell that plays beautiful music," Joy said.

"Music?" The goblin's eyes narrowed slyly. "Music that's good enough to win Jack Frost's competition?"

"Oh, yes!" Kirsty said.

"Listen." Joy held up the shell. Merry-go-round music tinkled out.

"You'd definitely win the competition with this shell," Rachel told him.

The goblin looked at them suspiciously. "My friend got into trouble when three pesky fairies tricked him and stole one of my master's shells. How do I know you're not playing a trick on me?"

"Us?" Rachel said, opening her eyes wide.

"We don't want to trick you," Kirsty said, trying to sound like she meant it. "We just want to help."

"Don't you want to win that competition?" added Joy. "Just think of the candy!"

"Sugary and delicious," Rachel said. "Sticky and sweet . . ."

It was too much for the greedy goblin. "Give me that shell!" he shouted. Throwing the conch shell to the ground, he grabbed the pointy shell and blew hard. Lively music echoed through the air.

The goblin's face lit up. "I'm going to win the competition!" he cried. "I'm going to get all the candy!" He hurried

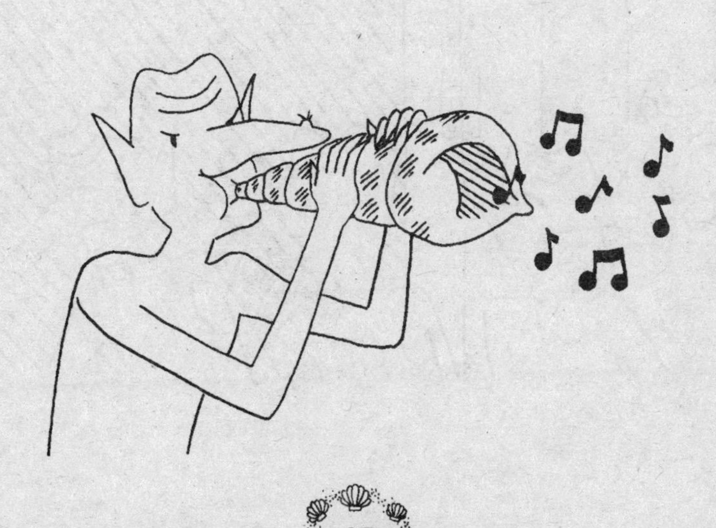

back to the other goblins. "Listen, everyone!"

The girls and Joy watched as the other goblins crowded around him while the shell played its magical music.

"Come on!" Rachel urged Joy and Kirsty. "Let's go, while they're busy!" She flew up into the air, but then

stopped. "Oh, no!" she exclaimed. "Look at the doorway!"

The goblins were all pushing and shoving to get into the castle. They all wanted to play their music for Jack Frost.

"We're never going to get in that way now!" Kirsty cried.

"What are we going to do?" Joy asked, frowning.

"You could always go a different way," Henry said.

He scuttled toward the castle walls and called, "Sally! Are you there? I have some friends who need your help!"

Kirsty and Rachel stared in surprise as a small brown-and-black beetle suddenly popped its head out of the sand.

"Hello!" the beetle said.

"Sally, these friends of mine are trying to rescue a magic shell from the tower," Henry explained.

"Pleased to meet you," Sally said. "Follow me!" Swinging around, she pushed her head against the castle wall and began to burrow. Her legs moved in a blur, and sand flew up all around. A few seconds later, she was gone, leaving a hole behind her.

"She made a tunnel!" Rachel gasped.

"Of course!" Joy beamed. "Sand beetles love burrowing through sand. Come on! Don't forget the conch shell!"

Rachel and Kirsty carried the shell over to the tunnel. Joy stopped to kiss the hermit crab. "Good-bye, Henry. See you soon."

"Bye, Henry," the girls called. "Good luck finding a shell!"

It was a tight squeeze in the tunnel. Rachel, Kirsty, and Joy pushed the shell in front of them. The sandy walls were rough against their knees and elbows.

"It's very dark," Kirsty puffed.

"I can fix that," Joy replied. She waved her wand and a glow lit up the dark, like sunlight.

"Almost there!" Sally called out from up ahead. "We can't go all the way to the top of the tower because the sand is too soft. But I can take you to a staircase that will lead you there."

Rachel and Kirsty looked at each other nervously. What if they bumped into

some goblins inside the castle, or, even worse, into Jack Frost himself?

A few minutes later, a circle of light appeared overhead.

"I'm out!" Sally called. "The coast is clear."

Rachel, Kirsty, and Joy scrambled to the end of the tunnel and stepped cautiously into a narrow hallway.

Opposite them, in the sandy wall, there was an arched doorway leading to some stairs. Floating down the stairs came the sounds of goblins blowing on shells and Jack Frost's voice snapping like broken ice.

"Useless! No! That won't do, either! No, that's useless, too. Is that the best you can do?"

Rachel shivered. "That staircase must lead up to Jack Frost's room. Do you think the goblin has played music from the enchanted shell yet?"

"It doesn't sound like it," said Joy.

"If you don't mind, I'm going to head back now," Sally said. "I don't like

goblins, with their big clumsy feet. My aunt nearly got squashed last week. Good luck!"

Waving a leg, she burrowed back into the wall.

"Thanks, Sally!" the girls and Joy called. Then they flew to the end of the hallway and found the stairs that led to the tower. They flew up them until they reached a big door at the top. Pushing it open, they peeked out.

"We're here!" Joy exclaimed.

"And there's Jack Frost's window!" Rachel hissed, pointing to the next tower over.

"Come on, let's swap the shells and get out of here," Kirsty said.

"But which one is the magic shell, again?" Rachel asked.

They looked at the conch shells. The sun was hidden behind the clouds. Without it, all of the shells looked exactly the same!

"I know a way to tell, even when the sun isn't out," Joy said. "All conch shells make a noise, except for the magic Rainspell Shell. It doesn't make a sound when you blow in it; it just makes the wind change."

The girls and Joy flew to the first shell. Pushing their hair out of their eyes, they began to blow into the conches.

Whoop! went the first shell that Kirsty chose.

Toot! blew Rachel's.

"Whoa!" cried Joy as a gust of wind almost whisked her off the tower. She grabbed at the nearest conch shell to

steady herself and blew into it. It made a loud noise like a foghorn.

"Oh, no!" Kirsty gasped, glancing down. "The goblins in the boats are looking this way!"

She was right. A few goblins were still bobbing around in the sea, and now they looked up. Some of them began to point and shout.

The girls and Joy flew frantically from shell to shell. They had to find the right one, and fast!

The goblins started to paddle toward the beach.

"We have to go!" Joy exclaimed.

Kirsty couldn't stand the thought of giving up when they were so close. She looked around desperately. Which one was the magic shell?

"Come on, Kirsty!" cried Joy.

Kirsty suddenly had an idea. "I know! Why don't you use your wand, like you did in the tunnel? The light that came from it then was just like sunlight. It might light up the magic shell!"

Joy grinned. "You're right!" She waved her wand. There was a loud tinkling sound, and the wand lit up with a golden glow. Joy swept the wand through the air, and the glow moved like a beam from a flashlight through the gray air. As the light fell on the shells, one near Kirsty began to sparkle.

"The magic conch shell!" Kirsty gasped, flying toward it. She blew into the shell, just to make sure.

The shell didn't make a sound.

"Rachel!" Kirsty cried. "We found the shell!"

"I know!" Rachel replied. "And look at the goblins!"

Kirsty looked down. The magic shell had made the wind on the beach whip up. The goblins started yelling as their boats were tossed on the waves.

"Did I just do that?" Kirsty said.

Joy nodded. "Quick! Let's swap the shells!"

Rachel pulled the magic shell out of the wall, and Kirsty stuck the new shell in its place. Hearts racing, they hurried back to the door and flew down the stairs. As they entered the empty hallway, they could see the hole in the wall where Sally's tunnel started.

Suddenly, Joy stopped in her tracks, and the girls nearly crashed into her.

The goblin with the warty nose had come running into the hallway. He carried the pointy shell under one arm and charged right at them!

Escape!

Rachel and Kirsty froze.

"I have the best shell and I'm going to get all the candy!" the goblin muttered, running toward them.

Joy gasped. "He hasn't seen us yet!" Grabbing Rachel's and Kirsty's arms, she pulled them up to the ceiling.

Licking his lips, the goblin charged through the door that led to Jack Frost's tower. The shell's music seemed to be slowing down, getting fainter every second, just like a real merry-go-round when it comes to a stop.

"The magic's about to wear off!" Joy exclaimed. "Come on, let's get out of here before Jack Frost realizes he's been tricked!" She dived into the tunnel.

"If we slide down, it'll be quicker," Joy called back over her shoulder.

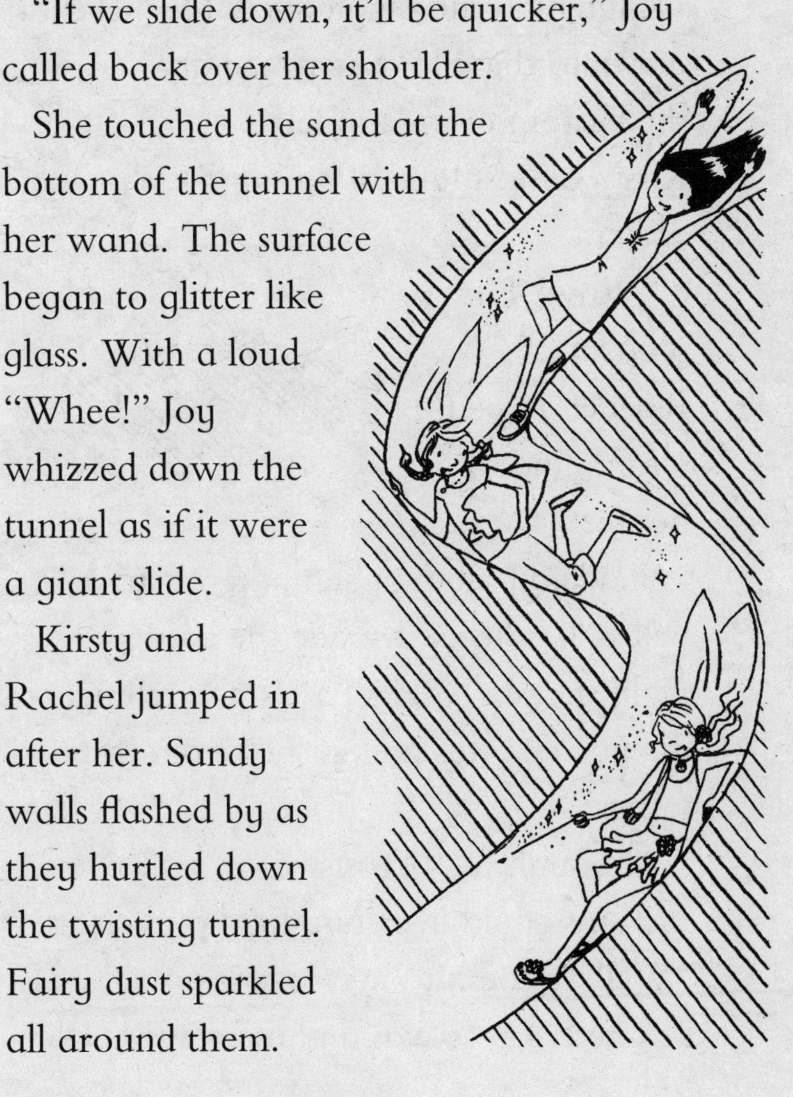

She touched the sand at the bottom of the tunnel with her wand. The surface began to glitter like glass. With a loud "Whee!" Joy whizzed down the tunnel as if it were a giant slide.

Kirsty and Rachel jumped in after her. Sandy walls flashed by as they hurtled down the twisting tunnel. Fairy dust sparkled all around them.

Clutching the magic shell, Rachel shot out onto the pile of seaweed at the bottom of the tunnel. Kirsty almost landed on top of her.

"Wow! That was amazing!" Rachel gasped, scrambling to her feet.

Suddenly, above them, there was a yell so loud that it made the castle walls shake. "WHAT?! You're telling me you got this useless shell from three fairies?"

Although Jack Frost was in his tower, the girls could hear him loud and clear. "Well, it doesn't make music now!" he shouted. There was a pause. "What do

you mean, you swapped it for a conch shell? A conch shell!"

"Quick!" Joy looked alarmed. "I think Jack Frost knows that we tricked the goblin!"

As the three friends flew up into the air, they saw Jack Frost storm to the window. "Pesky fairies!" he shouted. "Come back here with my magic shell!"

But he was too far away to stop them. With a final look at the castle, the girls and Joy flew away.

"Phew!" Rachel said as they reached the harbor at last. "That was scary!"

"Yes," Joy agreed. "But at least we rescued the second magic shell! Do you want to come to the underwater cave and help me put it back where it belongs?"

Kirsty looked at the boats bobbing on the calm sea. "We should get back to the regatta. We said we'd meet our moms to watch the race. They're probably waiting for us."

"Although it doesn't look like there's going to be a race," Rachel said with a sigh. "There's still not enough wind for the boats to sail."

"But as soon as I put the shell back, the wind will return," Joy reminded her.

Kirsty glanced at the big clock on the

harbor wall. Almost half an hour had passed since they had left their dads with the harbor master. "I don't think that's going to be fast enough. The

harbor master must be about to make a decision any minute now," she said, feeling disappointed.

"You mean, you need wind right now?" Joy asked.

Rachel and Kirsty nodded.

"No problem!" Joy exclaimed, grinning. She swooped down to a rock and raised the shell to her lips. At once, a breeze swirled across the beach.

"The shell's bringing back the wind!" Kirsty exclaimed.

Joy grinned and blew harder. With every breath, the wind grew stronger and stronger, until the sails of the boats were flapping in the breeze.

Lowering the shell, Joy smiled at Rachel and Kirsty. "I think your dads will be able to race now." She waved her wand and a cloud of sparkling fairy dust floated around them.

Kirsty and Rachel were their normal size again. "Thanks, Joy!" They grinned.

"Thank *you*," said the fairy. "I couldn't have found the shell without your help. See you soon!"

In the distance, there was a loud hooting noise. "The race is about to start!" Kirsty exclaimed. "Come on, Rachel!"

Waving good-bye to Joy, the two girls ran across the pebbly beach.

As they reached the ice cream truck and joined their moms, they heard the

horn again. The breeze swelled, and the boats shot across the starting line.

"Come on, Dad!" Rachel and Kirsty shouted as their dads' boat raced toward the finish line. Their boat was ahead of the others! The girls watched as the sail billowed in the wind. As they got closer and closer to the finish line, it looked like Mr. Tate and Mr. Walker were going to come in first. And . . .

"They won!" cheered Mrs. Tate.

Rachel beamed at Kirsty. "I'm very glad we got that shell back."

"Me, too," Kirsty agreed. "And now there's just one more shell to find."

Rachel grinned. "And when we get it back, Rainspell Island will be the perfect place for summer vacation again!"

The Magic
Scallop Shell

Contents

No Donkey Rides! 133

Summer Magic 139

Trapped! 147

A Friend's Help 159

The Underwater Cave 167

The sun was shining and a breeze was blowing fluffy white clouds across the sky as Rachel and Kirsty ran down to the beach. It was a perfect day to be outside!

"It's very quiet," said Kirsty. Usually there were lots of people out on Rainspell Island, playing, swimming, and sunbathing. But ever since Jack Frost had stolen the

sand and shells for his castle, people had been staying away from the beach.

Rachel nodded. "It just isn't the same without the sand. We have to get the last Rainspell Shell back." Just then, she spotted Mr. Williams and his four fluffy donkeys farther down the beach. Mr. Williams was holding up the smallest donkey's leg and checking its hoof. "But at least the donkeys are still here," Rachel added.

She and Kirsty headed over.

"Hello, Mr. Williams," Kirsty called. "Can we have a ride, please?"

Mr. Williams shook his head. "Not today, I'm afraid. The beach is too rocky. Pippin hurt her hoof stepping on a stone."

"Oh, no!" Kirsty stroked the donkey's velvety nose. "Will she be OK?"

"She'll be fine after a day's rest," Mr. Williams replied. "But there won't be any more donkey rides while the beach is like this." He sighed. "I'd better take them back to their field."

Rachel and Kirsty watched as Mr. Williams led the unhappy donkeys away.

"Jack Frost is determined to ruin everyone's vacation, isn't he?" Rachel said sadly.

Suddenly, Kirsty pointed to a tidepool. "Look! I saw some sparkles over there."

A cloud of golden dust whooshed up from behind a rock, and Joy the Summer Vacation Fairy spiraled into the air. "Hello!"

Joy landed on Kirsty's shoulder, light as a feather. "I've figured out where Jack Frost is keeping the magic scallop shell!" she exclaimed. "He's using it to decorate his throne in the Great Hall of his castle." Joy clasped her hands together. "It's going to be very difficult to rescue that shell. It's the trickiest one of all! But if we don't put it back in its underwater cave, the beaches on Rainspell Island will never have sand again."

"We can't let that happen!" said Rachel.

Kirsty nodded. "It might be dangerous, but we're not going to give up. We have to get that shell back!"

Joy waved her wand, showering Rachel and Kirsty with fairy dust. At once, they shrank down to fairy-size.

"It's not going to be easy to get into the castle this time," Joy warned the girls as they flew over the island. "Jack Frost is so angry about losing the other two shells that he put extra goblins on guard duty."

Sure enough, when they reached the castle, there were goblins everywhere — on the drawbridge and by the door, walking around the towers and patrolling the beach.

Kirsty noticed that the windows in the castle looked strange. She flew to a nearby window and touched the glass. It was freezing cold! "It's made of ice!" she gasped.

"All of the windows are," Joy replied. "Jack Frost has put a spell on them so they won't melt in the sun. My special summer magic can make a hole just big enough for us to get through." She looked nervously at the goblin guards below. "Should we fly to the back of the castle, where it's quieter?"

Rachel and Kirsty nodded, and they all flew around the castle. They stopped next to a small window near the bottom of a tower.

"Here goes!" Joy cried. Her wand glowed brightly as she touched it to the icy

window. There was a fizzing sound, and the ice began to melt around the tip of the wand.

"It's working!" Kirsty whispered.

"Keep going, Joy. It's almost big enough for us to fit through!" urged Rachel.

Concentrating hard, Joy made a perfectly round hole in the window. "Phew!" she said. She looked pale under her freckles.

"Are you OK?" Rachel asked.

Joy nodded. "I'm just tired. Jack Frost's spell is strong, and melting the ice is very difficult." She waved her wand. Usually a cloud of glittering fairy dust whooshed

out, but now only a few sparkles floated into the sky. "There's not much magic left in my wand," she said, looking worried. Joy began to squeeze through the hole. "Come on. Let's go rescue the last Rainspell Shell!"

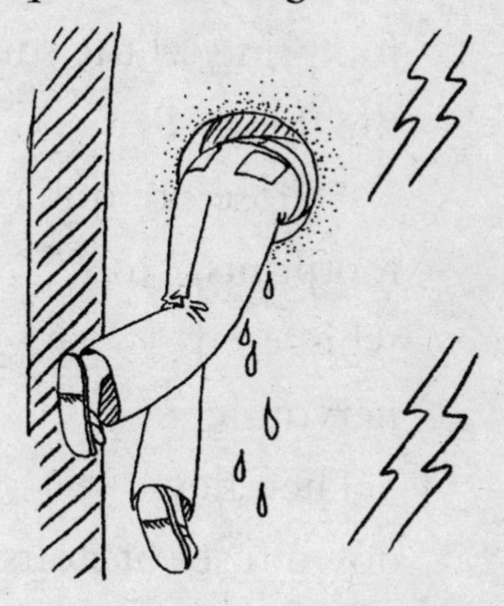

Rachel and Kirsty followed her through the window. It led into a narrow hallway.

"Be careful!" Joy whispered. "The Great Hall is this way."

The three of them flew cautiously along the hallway, staying near the ceiling where the shadows were darkest. Rachel could feel herself getting goose

bumps. What if a goblin came down the hall? Or, even worse, what if Jack Frost did?

There were large footprints in the sand on the floor.

"Those are goblin footprints," Joy whispered nervously.

They flew down a set of stairs and along another hallway until they came to a big wooden door.

"This is the door to the Great Hall," Joy told the girls.

Rachel pushed the door open a little and peeked in. "There's no one here," she said in relief.

A magnificent throne stood in the middle of the empty room. Icicles hung off its arms, and its back was a large scallop shell carved out of ice. A real scallop shell was stuck to the very top. Its wavy, white edge glowed with golden fairy dust.

"It's the magic shell," Joy breathed.

"Quick!" Kirsty said. "Let's grab it before anyone sees us!"

The three of them flew over and took hold of the shell. It came loose with the faintest sound of tinkling fairy music.

"Stop right there!" A cold voice snapped through the air.

Rachel, Kirsty, and Joy spun around. Jack Frost was standing in the doorway!

Trapped!

"Quick!" Rachel gasped. "We have to do something!"

Jack Frost raised his hands, but Joy was quicker. Waving her wand so that it flared like a candle, she pointed it at the sandy floor. There was a sizzling sound, and the floor glowed red-hot.

With a cry, Jack Frost leaped back. "Ow! The floor is hot." The icicles on his beard began to drip.

"Melt the window, Joy!" Kirsty cried. "Let the sunshine in!"

Joy raced to the window and touched the pane with her wand. There was a faint fizzing noise, and a very small patch on the window began to melt. "My wand is running out of magic!" Joy gasped.

"Freeze!" Jack Frost ordered, pointing his fingers at the floor.

Rachel watched in dismay as the red glow faded from the floor. "Quick, Joy!" she urged.

"Come on, wand!" Joy whispered. There was a sizzle and a loud snap as a maze of splinters spread across the ice.

Crack! The window shattered! Sunlight came streaming in.

Jack Frost stumbled backward with his hands over his eyes. "Guards!" he shouted.

"Let's go!" Kirsty said, flying into the air with Rachel. "Come on, Joy!"

But Joy didn't move. She lay on the window ledge, panting. Her face was

white, and her wand had lost all its sparkle.

Kirsty and Rachel swooped down and tried to help Joy up.

"Can't move . . ." Joy murmured. "Too tired . . . no magic left . . ."

"Don't worry," Rachel said, trying to stay calm. "We'll help you. Kirsty, can you take the shell while I carry Joy?"

Kirsty nodded. Rachel put her arms around the little fairy and flew upward, straining hard. Even though the fairy was tiny, it was very difficult to fly with her.

Joy hung limply, her wings drooping and her eyes closed.

"Guards!" Jack Frost yelled again.

"Quick, Rachel, through the window!" said Kirsty.

Jack Frost raised his hands, and a gust of freezing air filled the room. With a loud crackle, the window froze over with a fresh sheet of glittering ice.

Kirsty looked around desperately. There was a narrow staircase on the other side of the room. "Let's go that way!" she called to Rachel.

Carrying Joy and the shell, the two girls flew across the room and up the spiral staircase. Below, there was the sound of pounding feet and shouting. The goblins were coming!

"Stop those fairies, NOW!" Jack Frost yelled, and the goblins started to run up the stairs.

Kirsty spotted a window

ahead. "If Joy's wand hadn't used up all its magic, we could have melted our way out," she panted.

Just then, the two girls heard a faint scratching noise and a little voice singing, "All day long, I dig and dig. All day long, I dig and dig . . ."

"I know that voice!" Rachel gasped. "It's Sally, the sand beetle!"

A little brown-and-black beetle popped its head out of the wall.

"Hello again!" Sally said in surprise. "What are you doing here?"

She looked at Joy, and her eyes widened. "What happened?"

"It's a long story," Kirsty replied.

"We really need to get out of here, Sally!" Rachel said. "Fast!"

"Come here, you pesky fairies!" the goblins shouted as they charged up the staircase.

"Quick!" said Sally. "Follow me!"

Her legs whirred as she made the tunnel bigger. Kirsty dived in, hugging the shell in her arms. Rachel pulled Joy in behind her. They just made it before the goblins rushed around the corner. The girls held their breath

and stayed very still. Would the goblins notice the tunnel?

To their relief, the heavy footsteps thudded by and moved on up the stairs.

Kirsty and Rachel slithered through the tunnel with Joy and the magic shell. It led to a narrow window ledge on the other side of the castle wall.

"That was close!" Sally said, waving her feelers.

"Very," Kirsty agreed.

"We can't stay here," Rachel said, glancing at the window behind them. "The goblins might see us."

"Can't you fly away?" Sally asked.

Kirsty shook her head, trying not to look down. The beach was a long way below them! "We can't carry Joy and the shell that far."

"Oh, what are we going to do?" Rachel said desperately.

Caw!

They all jumped and looked up. A black-headed seagull was flying toward them.

"Do you fairies need some help?" it called.

A Friend's Help

The seagull looked as big as a horse, but its black eyes were kind.

"My name is Gregory," he cawed. "Is there something wrong with Joy?"

"She used up all her magic against Jack Frost," Rachel explained.

Joy groaned and her eyelids flickered.

"We need to take the magic scallop shell back to the underwater cave," said Kirsty.

"No problem," Gregory declared. "Climb on to my back and I'll fly you down to the sea."

The girls didn't need the seagull to tell them twice. Rachel scrambled on first with Joy, and Kirsty followed with the scallop shell. They dug their hands into

the soft white feathers on Gregory's back and held on tight.

At that moment, the goblins ran down the stairs. Gregory flapped his powerful wings and flew away from the window ledge. The goblins were too late!

"We're safe!" Rachel shouted as the wind swept through her hair.

"NO!" They turned and saw Jack Frost standing at the window of the Great

Hall. "You pesky fairies!" he yelled. "Bring back that shell!"

"Never!" Kirsty shouted back. She laughed happily as Gregory swooped over the sea.

"Oh, goodness," Joy mumbled, starting to wake up. "I don't feel very well. Everything's swaying."

"It's OK. We're on Gregory's back," Rachel told her. She squeezed Joy's hand. "We're safe now."

"I'm afraid I can only take you as far as the surface of the sea," Gregory called over his shoulder. "You'll need to swim the rest of the way to the cave."

Kirsty looked over at Rachel. "How are we going to do that? We can't breathe underwater."

"Don't worry," said Joy, trying to sit up. "We can use fairy magic."

"But your wand has run out of magic," Rachel reminded her.

"We don't need my wand," Joy replied. She was looking much better now. "What we need is this!" She rummaged in her beach bag and pulled out a sparkling pink bottle.

"It's a bottle of bubble mixture!" Kirsty said. Joy pulled out a small bubble wand with a circle at one end.

"It's fairy bubble mixture," said Joy. She dipped the bubble wand into the bottle and blew three big bubbles. She handed one to Rachel and one to Kirsty

and kept one for herself. "Put the bubble on your head."

The bubbles sank down over the girls' faces until their heads were completely enclosed. They looked just like old-fashioned diving helmets!

Joy put one on, too. Then she patted the seagull's smooth feathers. "Good-bye, Gregory. Thank you for rescuing us!" Holding on to the magic shell, she looked at Rachel and Kirsty. "Ready?"

They nodded nervously. The sea beneath them looked very deep!

"One, two, three . . . JUMP!" Joy cried.

Down, down, down, Rachel, Kirsty, and Joy went into the deep water. At first, the girls held their breath, but they soon realized they didn't need to. With the fairy helmets on, they could breathe underwater! Fairy magic also seemed to be keeping them warm, because the water didn't feel cold at all.

"Wow!" Kirsty said, gazing around. The ocean floor was covered with pink, peach, and white coral. Anemones waved their tentacles, and schools of brightly colored fish swam by.

"It's beautiful!" Rachel gasped.

Joy bobbed beside her, grinning. "Let's go to the cave." She gave a whistle, and three sparkling golden sea horses swam toward them. Bubbles trailed from their flared nostrils.

"They're wearing bridles!" Rachel exclaimed.

"Jump on!" said Joy. With one arm clutching the magic shell, she mounted the first sea horse.

The other two sea horses bobbed over to Rachel and Kirsty. The girls scrambled onto their backs, and the sea horses set

off. They whooshed through the water, dodging past seaweed and swerving around schools of fish. Rachel and Kirsty laughed out loud. It was the most exciting ride ever!

"Here's the cave!" Joy called at last.

A small underwater cave appeared ahead, hollowed out of the rocks. The surface of the sea was far above, glittering in the sun. Climbing off the sea horses, Rachel, Kirsty, and Joy swam into the cave.

The floor of the cave was covered with tiny, pink shells. Three stone shelves were mounted on the walls. On one shelf was the glittering twisty curly shell they had rescued from the castle drawbridge. On the next shelf was the glowing cream conch shell they had taken from the tower. The third shelf was empty.

"That's where this shell belongs," Joy

explained. She carefully propped the white scallop shell onto the shelf.

At once, a fountain of pink-and-gold sparkles fizzed into the water. The girls heard a low rumbling noise. It got louder and louder, filling the cave. It ended with a loud crash. Then there was silence.

"What was that?' Kirsty asked, taking her hands away from her ears.

Joy stared at her with wide eyes. "I think that was Jack Frost's castle falling down."

"Look at your wand, Joy!" Rachel gasped. The fairy's wand was glittering gold again, and sparkles trailed from the tip.

"My wand has filled up with fairy magic!" Joy cried in delight.

The three friends swam back to the sea horses and rode up to the surface of the sea.

"The castle's gone!" said Kirsty, staring at the cove where Jack Frost's castle had been.

There was nothing left at all, just a thick layer of soft, yellow sand on the beach.

Joy, Rachel, and Kirsty said good-bye to the sea horses and, shaking their wings dry, flew into the air. The bubbles on their heads popped as they soared up.

"Look! Someone wrote something in the sand!" Rachel pointed to the beach where the castle had been.

Large spiky letters spelled out: YOU CAN'T CATCH ME!

"It looks like Jack Frost got away," said Kirsty.

Joy nodded. "But that doesn't matter right now. The important thing is whether Rainspell Island has its summer vacation magic back. Let's go and see!"

They flew to the other side of the island.

"Look!" Rachel gasped. Golden sand stretched from the white cliffs down to the blue sea. Tidepools glittered in the sun, and the beach was dotted with shells in every color of the rainbow.

Children laughed and shouted as they ran across the sand with pails and shovels. By the harbor, Rosie's ice cream truck tinkled a merry tune, and Mr. Williams led his donkeys back down to the beach.

"Thank you so much for helping me get Rainspell's summer vacation magic back," Joy said, giving Kirsty and Rachel each a hug.

"Of course," Rachel said smiling.

"I'm just glad we could help," Kirsty added. "It's been a lot of fun." She

looked out at the beach. "There are our moms and dads!" The Walkers and the Tates were heading down the path with towels, beach bags, and a picnic basket.

The girls and Joy flew down to the beach. Joy waved her wand, and the girls shot back up to their normal size.

"Bye, Joy," Kirsty said. "We'll miss you and your summer magic."

Joy grinned. "Don't worry, you haven't seen the last of it yet." She twirled around. "Bye!" she called, darting away in a cloud of golden sparkles.

"Hi, girls!" Mr. Walker called. "Isn't it great? The wind blew all the sand back on to the beach again! It was like magic!"

Rachel and Kirsty grinned at each other.

"Let's have our picnic over here," Mrs. Tate said, starting to unpack. There were sandwiches, apples, juicy red strawberries, chips, and bottles of soda.

"This looks delicious," Kirsty said, helping to put out some plates.

"I'd like to take a swim before lunch," Rachel said.

"Me, too!" Kirsty agreed.

"Well, we've brought your beach bags with us," Mrs. Walker said. "Why don't you get changed?"

The girls nodded and took their beach bags behind a large rock.

"Oh!" Rachel gasped as she opened her bag. "Look!" She pulled out a beautiful bathing suit. It was pink and purple, and shimmered with silver glitter.

Kirsty looked in her bag. "I have one, too! They must be a magic present from Joy to say thank you!"

"I'm so glad Rainspell Island is back to normal," Rachel said as they changed into their new bathing suits. "Now this is going to be the best vacation ever!"

"It really is," Kirsty agreed.

Shouting and laughing, the two girls ran across the sand, which seemed softer and more golden than ever before, and splashed into the sparkling sea.

RAINBOW magic™

THE RAINBOW FAIRIES

Find the magic in every book!

RAINBOW magic

These activities are magical!

Play dress-up, send friendship notes, and much more!

SCHOLASTIC

www.scholastic.com

www.rainbowmagiconline.com

RMACTIV3